Paddington

This edition published in paperback by HarperCollins Children's Books in 2014
First published in hardback by HarperCollins Publishers, USA in 1988
First published in hardback in Great Britain by Collins in 1998
First published in paperback by Picture Lions in 1999
Revised edition published in 2007
This edition published as part of a set in 2017

1 3 5 7 9 10 8 6 4 2

ISBN: 978-0-00-794313-5

Collins and Picture Lions are imprints of the Children's Division, part of HarperCollins Publishers Ltd.
HarperCollins Children's Books is a division of HarperCollins Publishers Ltd.

Text copyright © Michael Bond 1998, 2007
Illustrations copyright © R. W. Alley 2007

Visit our website at: www.harpercollins.co.uk

Printed and bound in China

Michael Bond
Paddington

The original story of the bear from Peru

Illustrated by R. W. Alley

HarperCollins *Children's Books*

Mr and Mrs Brown first met Paddington on a railway platform. In fact, that was how he came to have such an unusual name for a bear, because Paddington was the name of the station.

The Browns were waiting to meet their daughter, Judy, when Mr Brown noticed something small and furry near the LEFT LUGGAGE office. "It looks like a bear," he said.

"A bear?" repeated Mrs Brown. "On Paddington Station? Don't be silly, Henry. There can't be!"

But Mr Brown was right. It was sitting on an old leather suitcase marked WANTED ON VOYAGE, and as they drew near it stood up and politely raised its hat.

"Good afternoon," it said. "May I help you?"

"It's very kind of you," said Mr Brown, "but as a matter of fact, we were wondering if we could help *you*?"

"You're a very small bear," said Mrs Brown. "Where are you from?"

The bear looked around carefully before replying.

"Darkest Peru. I'm not really supposed to be here at all. I'm a stowaway."

"You don't mean to say you've come all the way from South America on your own?" exclaimed Mrs Brown. "Whatever did you do for food?"

Unlocking the suitcase, the bear took out an almost empty glass jar. "I ate marmalade," it said. "Bears like marmalade."

Mrs Brown looked at the label around the bear's neck.
It said, quite simply,

PLEASE LOOK AFTER THIS BEAR. Thank you.

"Oh, Henry!" she cried. "We can't leave him here all by himself. There's no knowing what might happen to him. Can't he come home and stay with us?"

"Stay with us?" repeated Mr Brown nervously.

He looked down at the bear. "Er, would you like that?" he asked. "That is," he added hastily, "if you have nothing else planned."

"Oooh, yes," replied the bear. "I would like that very much. I've nowhere to go and everyone seems in such a hurry."

"That settles it," said Mrs Brown. "Now, you must be thirsty after your journey. Mr Brown can get you some tea while I go and meet our daughter, Judy."

"But, Mary," said Mr Brown. "We don't even know its name."

Mrs Brown thought for a moment. "I know," she said. "We'll call him Paddington – after the station."

"Paddington!" The bear tested it several times to make sure. "It sounds very important."

Mr Brown tried it out next. "Follow me, Paddington," he said. "I'll take you to the snack bar."

Mr Brown was as good as his word. Paddington had never seen so many snacks on one tray and he didn't know which to try first.

He was so hungry and thirsty he climbed up on the table to get a better look.

Mr Brown turned away, pretending he had tea with a bear on Paddington Station every day of his life.

"Henry!" cried Mrs Brown, when she arrived with Judy.
"What *are* you doing to that poor bear?"

Paddington jumped up to raise his hat, and in his haste,
he trod on a strawberry tart, skidded on the cream and fell
over backwards into his cup of tea.

"I think we'd better go before anything else happens," said Mr Brown.

Judy took hold of Paddington's paw. "Come along," she said. "We'll take you home and you can meet Mrs Bird and my brother, Jonathan."

Mr Brown led the way to a waiting taxi. "Number thirty-two Windsor Gardens, please," he said.

The driver stared at Paddington. "Bears is extra," he growled. "Sticky bears is twice as much. And make sure none of it comes off on my interior. It was clean when I set out this morning."

The sun was shining as they drove out of the station, and there were cars and big red buses everywhere. Paddington waved to some people waiting at a bus stop, and several of them waved back. It was all very friendly.

Paddington tapped the taxi driver on his shoulder. "It isn't a bit like Darkest Peru," he announced.

The man jumped at the sound of Paddington's voice. "Cream!" he said bitterly. "Cream and jam all over me coat!" He slid the little window behind him shut.

"Oh, dear, Henry," murmured Mrs Brown. "I wonder if we're doing the right thing?"

Fortunately, before anyone had time to answer, they arrived at Windsor Gardens and Judy helped Paddington on to the pavement.

"Now you're going to meet Mrs Bird," she said. "She looks after us. She's a bit fierce at times, but she doesn't really mean it. I'm sure you'll like her."

Paddington felt his knees begin to wobble. "I'm sure I shall, if you say so," he replied.
"The thing is, will she like me?"

"Goodness gracious!" exclaimed Mrs Bird. "What *have* you got there?"

"It's not a what," said Judy. "It's a bear called Paddington and he's coming to stay with us."

"A bear," said Mrs Bird, as Paddington raised his hat. "Well, he has good manners, I'll say that for him."

"I'm afraid I stepped on a jam tart by mistake," said
Paddington.

"I can see that," said Mrs Bird. "You'd better have a bath
before you're very much older. Judy can turn it on for you. I
daresay you'll be wanting some marmalade, too!"

"I think she likes you," whispered Judy.

Paddington had never been in a bathroom before and while the water was running he made himself at home. First of all, he tried writing his new name in the steam on the mirror.

Then he used Mr Brown's shaving foam to draw a map of Peru on the floor.
It wasn't until a drip landed on his head that he remembered what he was supposed to be doing.

He soon discovered
that getting into a
bath is one thing, but
it's quite another
matter getting out
again – especially when
it's full of soapy water.

Paddington tried calling out, "Help!" – at first in a quiet voice so as not to disturb anyone, then very loudly,

"HELP!

HELP!"

When that didn't work, he began baling the water out with his hat. But the hat had several holes in it, and his map of Peru soon turned into a sea of foam.

Suddenly, Jonathan and Judy burst into the bathroom and
lifted a dripping Paddington on to the floor.

"Thank goodness you're all right!" cried Judy. "We heard
you calling out."

"Fancy making such a mess," said Jonathan admiringly.
"You should have pulled the plug out."

"Oh!" said Paddington. "I never
thought of that."

When Paddington came downstairs, he looked so clean no one could possibly be cross with him. His fur was all soft and silky, his nose gleamed and his paws had lost all traces of the jam and cream.

The Browns made room for him in a small armchair, and
Mrs Bird brought him a pot of tea and a plate of hot
buttered toast and marmalade.

"Now," said Mrs Brown, "you must tell us all about yourself. I'm sure you must have had lots of adventures."

"I have," said Paddington earnestly. "Things are always happening to me. I'm that sort of a bear." He settled back in the armchair.

"I was brought up by my Aunt Lucy in Darkest Peru," he began. "But she had to go into a Home for Retired Bears in Lima." He closed his eyes thoughtfully and a hush fell over the room as everyone waited expectantly.

After a while, when nothing happened, they began to get restless. Mr Brown tried coughing. Then he reached across and poked Paddington.

"Well I never," he said. "I do believe he's fast asleep!"

"After all that's happened to him," said Mrs Brown, "is it any wonder?"